For Mitch, as always

ONE

Inside the school, the bomb squad tried to find a bomb that could go off at any moment. Police cars and fire trucks surrounded the building. Their emergency lights blazed in the dreary light of this winter afternoon. I shivered from cold as I waited beside the cop cars.

The students had been evacuated. They now stood in the snow-covered sports field below the school. The kids knew someone had made a bomb threat. They were also watched over by their teachers. So I was surprised to see a teenage boy run into a side entrance of the school. He wore a red hoodie with a black skull on the back.

"Hey, stop!" I cried. Then I turned to the nearest cop, Officer Banks. "A kid just ran inside."

"We have things under control," Banks said. "All the students have been evacuated."

"There's a boy in that building," I insisted. "If that school blows, he'll die!"

The cop turned his back on me. When I tried to tell him again, he ignored me as if I wasn't there.

I tried the firefighters. "There's a kid in there!" But they also acted as if I was invisible.

I bolted inside the school after the kid, hoping to stop him. The rows of lockers seemed to go on forever as I raced from room to room. I had only minutes to find the boy and get out of this building before it blew.

Yet as I turned the corner to race down another hallway, I saw a janitor calmly mopping the floor. "Can I help you?" he said.

"What are you doing here?" I yelled as I ran toward him. "There's a bomb. This place is about to explode!"

The janitor looked at me blankly.

"Didn't you see the cops and their sniffer dog?" I asked him. "They cleared the building. They're trying to track down the bomb before it goes off."

"Why are *you* here then?" he asked me.

"I followed a kid inside. Did he run this way?"

"You shouldn't be here."

Yeah, I thought, tell me something I don't know. "I tried to tell the cops the boy was here, but they wouldn't believe me." I started off again down the hall. "I've got to find him." I glanced back briefly as I called, "Get the hell out of here!"

"I can help," the janitor said, but he didn't run after me. He just stood there in his gray uniform, holding the mop. Even so, as I turned the corner and started down the next hallway, I heard him repeat himself. He sounded as if he were right behind me. "I can help."

Then the boom of the explosion sounded, throwing me to the floor. A moment later a ball of fire shot down the hallway toward me. I knew in that instant, before the searing heat hit, that I would certainly die.

TWO

"**N**o!" I cried, sitting upright in bed. I blinked into the dark, confused. Where was I? Only a moment ago I'd been running down the high-school hallway, trying to save a kid. Then the school exploded around me. I was so sure I was about to die.

"What?" Matt said. "Claire, what's the matter?" He turned on the lamp on the bedside table. We'd been dating for a couple of months. He'd slept over after our date the night before.

"What is it?" he asked again.

"There was a bomb. The high school exploded! Oh my god, Matt. There was a kid in there with me!"

"It was just a dream, a nightmare."

"A dream? No, it was all so real. A boy charged into the school, like he was on a mission. I searched the school, but I couldn't see him anywhere." I ran a hand through my mess of curls, trying to remember. The dream was already starting to fade. "There was a janitor too."

"A janitor?"

"He was in the building with me before it exploded. He said he could help me."

"Well, I imagine he could." Matt grinned as he glanced around my bedroom. Clothes were scattered across the floor. "You sure could use a janitor in this place."

He had a point. My one-bedroom apartment was cluttered. I had very little storage space, so I ended up piling my things on the floor. I needed a bigger place.

"Matt, the dream felt so real." I reached for my cell on the nightstand. "I've got to phone my editor. Maybe she's heard something."

I worked for the *Black Lake Times*. Carol and I were the only two reporters at this small-town newspaper. We regularly phoned each other at home if we heard about a story.

Matt took my phone and put it back on the nightstand. "It's three o'clock in the morning. You can't phone Carol now. Claire, you're taking this dream far too seriously. It *was* just a dream."

I fell back on my pillow. "But I was *there*. And I felt so helpless. The police wouldn't listen to me. When I said there was a kid in the building, they ignored me."

"The cops would never do that." Matt leaned on his elbow to face me. "Look, your mind is just working through these visions you've been having. You know the cops

7

never take your mom's visions seriously. You're scared they'll judge you too."

Matt was right, of course. My mom had made a habit of telling the police about her visions. She'd think she knew where a lost child was, or where a body would be found. But she was often wrong. The child or the body would be found in another place.

The police were polite to Mom at first. Now they wouldn't take her calls. They thought she was crazy.

The trouble was, over the past winter I'd suddenly started having visions too. That was how Matt and I had ended up together. Matt was the search-and-rescue manager for our area. I'd told him about my vision of a girl named Amber Miller. I was sure she wasn't just lost. She had been kidnapped. In the end, it turned out I was right.

At first Matt thought *I* was crazy, but I won him over. We ended up dating after that. Well, after I broke things off with a certain firefighter. But all that was history now. I had definitely fallen for Matt. I felt a thrill run through me as I looked at his handsome face.

"You know what's strange about my visions?" I asked.

Matt laughed. "That you're having them?"

I shook my head. "My mom only ever has visions of the present. She holds an object that belongs to a person and sees a vision of what's happening to the owner right then."

"Yeah, so?"

"When you and your team were searching the forest for Amber Miller, my visions were taking place in the present too. When I saw those fires that Trevor set, I saw visions of the *past*."

Matt held back a yawn. "I don't understand what you're getting at."

"Now I think I'm seeing into the future."

"You don't know that."

"Yes," I said, "I do. Someone *will* set a bomb in that high school. Matt, if I don't stop him, I'm sure the school will explode."

"Why are you so certain?"

I shook my head. I didn't know why. I just *knew*.

"I've got to warn the cops," I said, reaching for my cell again.

Matt put his hand on mine to stop me from phoning. "And what are you going to tell the police? That you had a dream the school would blow up? Claire, you know what they're going to say."

"That I'm as nutty as my mom."

He nodded. "You've built a reputation in this town. Don't ruin it like your mom ruined hers."

"But Matt, what if I'm right? What if someone *is* planting a bomb in that school? Think of the kids, all those lives in danger. What if I could prevent the explosion from happening?"

"And how would you do that? Do you know who will set the bomb?"

I thought back to the dream. I had seen the kid running into the building. Then I saw a janitor washing the floor. I felt the boom of the explosion as the flames rushed toward me.

"No," I said. "But that boy ran into the school just before it exploded. He was up to something. I suppose he could have been the bomber."

"Do you know the kid?"

"No."

"Come here." Matt wrapped his strong arms around me. "It was just a dream, a silly nightmare."

I nestled into his muscular chest. I felt so safe in his arms that I could almost believe he was right.

"You'll forget all about it by morning," he said.

I sighed. Morning couldn't come soon enough.

THREE

I stumbled into work early, carrying a cup of coffee. I hadn't slept after that terrible dream, though Matt snored the rest of the night. I kept rolling what I remembered of the nightmare over in my mind. Was the kid in the dream the bomber? Was the janitor? Why did the janitor tell me he could help me? Why had Officer Banks ignored my warning?

Little about the dream made sense. Yet I knew from my familiar gut feeling that I was right. I *had* dreamed of the future.

I set my coffee on my desk and fell into my chair, cradling my head in my hands. If I phoned the cops about the dream, I knew they would laugh at me. I didn't know what to do.

"Rough night?" Carol asked.

I looked up to see my editor at her desk. "You could say that," I said. Lost in thought, I hadn't seen her when I entered. Carol was chubby, and her hair was frizzy from bleaching, but she had a kind face.

"Did Matt keep you up all night again?" she asked.

I grinned sideways at her. "Only until midnight."

"Huh. I find that hard to believe." She looked over the rumpled dress shirt and slacks I'd pulled from the dryer. I hadn't had time to iron them that morning. "You look like you didn't sleep a wink last night."

I glanced at the small mirror on the wall beside my desk. My curly hair was a tangled mess. I hadn't been able to tame it that morning. My brown eyes were ringed with fatigue. Usually I looked younger than my age, thirty-one. Not this morning.

I sighed. "I had a nightmare and couldn't get back to sleep."

Carol sat forward, interested. "What kind of nightmare? Was it one of your visions?"

I had told Carol how my visions helped me catch a kidnapper and a firebug. But I knew I couldn't trust what I thought I saw in these visions. I was often wrong, jumping to conclusions. I had got an innocent kid arrested.

"It's probably nothing," I said, waving a hand. "Nothing but a silly dream."

I sipped my coffee, hoping Carol would drop the subject. Matt was right. I had to be careful what I said about the dream.

I wasn't about to tell Carol I was now dreaming of the future. If word got out about that, everyone in town would be asking me for lottery numbers.

Carol eyed me a moment, then sat back. "Well, I need you to pull yourself together and get up to the high school right away."

I stood, alarmed. "The high school?"

"Some kid tweeted a bomb threat against the school this morning."

"Oh my god," I said. I felt sick. Was my nightmare really happening?

"What was that boy thinking?" Carol asked. "He's scared all those kids at that school, not to mention their parents. And for what? The thrill of seeing the fire trucks arrive with their lights on? The cops with their sniffer dog?"

"So you don't believe there really is a bomb."

"No, of course not. There's been a wave of bomb threats across the country.

In almost every case, a kid made the threat on social media. It was always just a prank."

"I think there may be a bomb this time," I said.

"Why? You hear something? You know who made that bomb threat?"

"No, this is the first I've heard of it." Sort of, I thought.

"Then what?"

I hesitated. "In that dream I had, the school exploded."

Carol smiled, but not unkindly. "The school won't explode."

"I can't shake this feeling that it will," I said. I grabbed my camera bag. "Maybe I can stop it from happening."

"But how?"

"I don't know." I felt the emotion catch in my throat. "But I have to try. I must have had that dream for a reason. If I don't find a way to stop that bomber, a lot of lives will be lost." Including my own, I thought.

FOUR

When I reached the school, I felt I had stepped back into my nightmare. Police cars and fire trucks surrounded the school. The cops had already evacuated the students. The kids waited with their teachers on the snow-covered sports field.

Instead of trying to warn Officer Banks as I had in my dream, I went straight to Fire Chief Wallis. Jim was a family friend. My visions had helped him catch a firebug. I thought he might believe me.

The chief stood next to one of the fire trucks, dressed in full firefighting gear.

"The kids should be farther back," I said. "They could be hit by debris if a bomb goes off."

"You telling me how to do my job again?" The chief elbowed me in the ribs to let me know he was joking. "They're fine, Claire. And I doubt there is a bomb."

"I'm not so sure about that."

He lost his grin. "You know something I don't?"

I paused. "Maybe," I said.

"You had another one of your hunches?"

"I dreamed the school exploded."

"Damn." He turned back to the school. "Well, there's nothing you can do now. The cops are in there with the sniffer dog."

"But the bomb would be well hidden, right?"

"The dog is trained to smell explosives. If there is a bomb, the officer and his dog will find it."

"If they're not too late."

Just then I saw the boy from my dream run into the side entrance of the school. He wore a red hoodie with a black skull on the back. "That's him!" I cried. "That's the kid I saw in my dream."

"What kid?" Jim asked. He clearly hadn't seen him.

In my dream, I had wasted time trying to convince the cops and firefighters to follow the kid inside. Instead, I ran toward the school right away.

"Claire!" Jim called after me. "What are you doing?"

I turned briefly. "I've got to stop that kid."

"Claire, stop! You can't go in there!"

But I was already pushing open the side door to the school.

I sprinted down the hallway, looking into each classroom. I felt certain the bomb was about to go off any minute, as it had in my dream. I felt that eerie feeling like

I had lived this moment before. I *had*, in my nightmare.

As I turned the corner, I saw a janitor mopping the floor. He was the same man I'd seen in my dream. When he saw me he looked as surprised as I felt. He stopped to lean on the handle of his mop as I ran toward him. "Can I help you?" he asked me.

"What are you doing here?" I asked. "There was a bomb threat."

Again I felt a shiver run through me. This conversation was strangely like the one I'd had with him in my dream the night before.

"The cops said I could go ahead and wipe up this mess." He pointed at the boot and dog tracks that muddied the floor. "The sniffer dog didn't find a bomb. They're going let the kids back in shortly."

"They can't do that!" I turned to look down the hall. "Did you see a boy run this way?"

"One of the students? He shouldn't be in here, not yet."

Yeah, I thought, tell me something I don't know. I started off again down the hall. "I've got to find him." I glanced back briefly as I called, "Get the hell out of here!"

The janitor didn't turn to leave. He just stood there in his gray uniform, holding the mop as he stared after me.

I realized that in the dream, this was the moment the bomb went off. This was the instant I died.

I ran toward the exit, following the route I had taken in the dream. I hoped to God both the kid and the janitor had the sense to get themselves out. But when I reached the door, a cop blocked my way. He was Officer Banks, the cop from my dream. From my work at the paper, I knew most of the cops in town.

"What are you doing in here?" he demanded. "We aren't allowing anyone in yet."

"I followed a kid in here. I was trying to get him out."

The cop paused as if he found that suspicious. "Do you know his name?"

I shook my head. "He was in his mid teens. Not much taller than me. Skinny. He was wearing a red hoodie with a skull on the back."

"We'll take a look for him. In the meantime, I must ask you to leave." He held the door open for me, but I didn't go outside. I had to stop him from allowing the students back into the school.

"I understand you didn't find a bomb."

"That's right."

"The kid I saw seemed to be on a mission." I paused, aware I was about to accuse the kid without proof. In the past, I had gotten an innocent teen in trouble by misreading my visions. "What if that kid went back in to set a bomb after you finished your sweep?"

"And why would you think that?" he asked me. He smirked. "Did you see it in one of your visions?"

So he had heard about my second sight and clearly didn't believe in it. I hesitated. "A dream," I said finally.

The cop appeared annoyed. "Look, most of these bomb scares are just pranks," he said. "But we have to check, to be on the safe side."

"Then check again," I said. "That kid ran in here *after* you searched the school with the sniffer dog."

"I asked you to wait outside," he said.

I put a hand on his arm. "Please, you've got to take this seriously. The lives of all these kids are at risk."

Officer Banks looked down at my hand until I removed it from his arm. "I take this bomb threat *very* seriously," he said. I understood. It was *me* he didn't take seriously. He strode back down the hallway.

I stood at the door for a moment longer, unsure what to do. I had no idea who the bomber was or where he was. But I was certain a bomb would go off in that school. Officer Banks wouldn't listen to me. I had to find someone who would.

FIVE

I ran from the school with my heart pounding in my throat. I was afraid the building was about to blow up behind me. When I turned the corner of the school, I ran right into Fire Chief Wallis.

"Whoa there, Claire!" he said, holding my shoulders to stop me from falling. "What the hell were you doing in the school?"

I struggled to catch my breath. "That boy I ran after. I think he may have set the bomb. Why else would I dream about him?"

"But the cops haven't found a bomb. They're about to let the kids back in the school."

"I know. I just talked to Officer Banks. Chief, for god's sake, don't let them send the kids back in that building!"

Jim eyed me, puzzled. "What's going on, Claire? I've never seen you like this."

"The building is going to blow. I *know* it is."

To my surprise, Jim didn't try to talk me out of the idea, as both my editor and Matt had—at least, not right away. "And you think you know who's responsible?" he asked. "That kid you chased into the building?"

"Yes. Chief, I know he was up to something."

"Maybe he *really* had to use the washroom." Jim grinned, trying to joke me out of my panic.

"Jim, in my dream the school exploded right after that kid ran into the building."

"So it should have blown by now, right? Come on, Claire. You're making yourself crazy. The bomb threat was just some stupid kid's prank."

The chief looked past me as his attention was drawn to someone approaching. I turned to see a girl in her mid teens walking toward us from the back of the fire truck. She was pretty and blond and wore a stylish fake-fur coat and pink beanie. Her family obviously had money.

"Excuse me," she said to the chief. "I'm sorry to interrupt, but I heard you talking." Then she turned to me. "You're right about Tyler."

"So you know who the bomber is? Is that his name? Tyler?"

She nodded. "He's the kid you chased into the school. I'm sure he made the bomb threat." She paused. "I don't know anything about a bomb though. I mean, a real bomb. *Is* there a bomb?"

Jim stepped in. "The police used the sniffer dog to sweep the school. The building is clean." He squeezed my arm, warning me to be quiet. "There is no bomb," he assured the girl.

"When you chased Tyler into the school, I figured you already knew he made that threat, or I would have said something earlier." She turned back to the chief. "I overheard Tyler in the hallway talking about a bomb scare at another school, something he saw online. He thought the bomb squad and the fire trucks were cool. He was trying to talk the other kid into pulling off something like that here."

I took out my notepad and scribbled a few notes. "Is Tyler a friend of yours?" I asked.

"My science teacher forced me to be his lab partner. But I never talk to him outside of class. He doesn't talk much to anyone, really. At noon he just hangs out in the basement with his dad."

"His dad?"

"The janitor."

I felt that chill run through me again. The kid was the janitor's son. I had dreamed of both Tyler and his dad.

"You'll let the cops know?" the girl asked.

"Stay here," Jim said. "I'll tell Officer Banks your story. I'm sure he'll want to talk to you."

"I may have more questions for you myself," I said. "What's your name? How can I reach you?"

"Ashley," she said. I added her name and cell number to the contact list on my phone.

Ashley stepped back to wait by the fire truck, her hands in her jeans pockets. I started to follow Jim to the school, but he held out a hand. "I think it's best if you wait here as well," he said.

"Because you don't think the cops will listen to me."

The chief held my gaze for a moment, then nodded. "Let me do the talking for you."

He headed toward the school, and I called after him. "Jim, what if I'm right?" I glanced back at Ashley. I didn't want to alarm her by mentioning the bomb again, but I couldn't let this go. "What if there really is a bomb?"

"I'll make sure the cops do another sweep," the chief said. "We won't let the kids in until we're sure it's safe. Okay?"

I nodded. "Okay." Yet his words didn't calm me. I was getting that sick feeling that always meant something was about to go terribly wrong.

SIX

I tried to look calm for Ashley's sake as we watched the cops through the school windows. One of them led a sniffer dog from classroom to classroom. "Do you really think there is a bomb?" Ashley asked me.

I shook my head. "Jim is right. In most cases, a bomb scare at a school is just a prank." There was no point scaring her further. "Can you tell me anything else about Tyler?" I asked. "You said he was your lab partner."

Ashley shrugged. "I don't know. He seemed out of it this past year, depressed.

The only thing he really got into were the rockets we built in class. He even bought more to set off at home."

"Model rockets? Don't you use gunpowder to launch them, like in fireworks?"

"It's not gunpowder exactly," she said. "Gunpowder explodes. The rocket fuel is made of the same three chemicals as gunpowder, but they're mixed differently. That way the rocket fuel burns, moving the rocket upward. If you used gunpowder, the rocket would explode on the launchpad."

"But those same chemicals could be mixed to create gunpowder and an explosion."

"I guess."

"And there must be some way to fire up the rocket safely, from a distance?"

"Sure, the igniter. Toy rockets come with them. We also learned how to hook up the igniter to a digital timer, so we could count down to a launch."

"So I imagine Tyler would have nearly everything he needs to make a pipe bomb right there," I said, mostly to myself. Then I realized my mistake.

Ashley's voice rose in panic. "You really do think there's a bomb in the school, don't you?"

"I'm just trying to get all the facts," I said. "If someone makes a bomb threat, there's always a slim chance he might follow through."

"But the cops and the dog *would* find the bomb, right?"

"As long as the dog is in the same room as the bomb, so it can smell the explosives." When Ashley's eyes widened, I added, "I'm sure the police will do a careful sweep."

Ashley bit her nail as she watched the cop and sniffer dog move to the next classroom.

"How about that kid you saw Tyler talking to in the hall?" I asked her. "Do you know his name? If we can track him down, he can back up your story about Tyler planning a bomb threat. Or maybe he's involved too."

"Spider. He's that kid over there, the one with the pierced lip."

I looked over at the boy, who was dressed all in black. Even his hair was dyed black. His eyes were rimmed with black eyeliner. The ring through his lip glinted when he elbowed the kid next to him and laughed.

"His name is Spider?" I asked.

"That's what he calls himself. Everyone does. I don't know if that's his real name or not."

"I'll go talk to him," I said. But just then Jim left the school and came back to the fire truck. I waited for him.

"Ashley, go to the office," he said. "Officer Banks will talk to you there before the assembly."

Ashley nodded and jogged into the school.

"What's going on?" I asked the chief. "Why are you letting Ashley into the school?"

"They're letting all the kids back in."

"Jim, no!"

"The school is clean. There is no bomb."

"How about the kid I saw running into the school? Tyler, the janitor's son?"

"The cops haven't found him yet."

"They have to find him before they let the kids back in. Jim, you can't let this happen."

"Claire, the threat is over. There is no bomb."

"But Jim—"

"Let it go."

"At least get Banks to talk to that kid over there, the one with the pierced lip. Ashley says Tyler tried to talk him into making the bomb threat."

"Ashley is likely telling Banks all that herself right now. Claire, let the cops do their job. They don't need your help."

I crossed my arms as I watched the teachers herd the kids back into the school. The cops didn't believe me. The chief didn't believe me. I had no proof that a bomb would go off in that school. All I had was a sick feeling in my stomach, a gut instinct that convinced me the explosion in the dream *would* happen. I just didn't know when.

"The school staff are taking the kids directly into the gym for an assembly," Jim said. "Officer Banks is going to explain to them how dangerous it is to make a bomb threat. He's asked our firefighting team to stand with him."

"I should come in. Take a few photos for the paper."

"Fine, but stay clear of Officer Banks. He isn't too pleased with you right now—or me, for that matter."

"But I was only trying to help."

"I tried to explain how your visions have solved crimes in the past. Banks brushed it off but searched the school again anyway. Now he feels we wasted time and money."

The last of the students filed into the school. "We'd better get in there," I said.

"You behave yourself." The chief gave me a stern look. "I don't want to hear any more about the school exploding. You'll scare the kids."

I followed Jim inside and took a few photos of Officer Banks as he lectured the kids. The other cops and firefighters stood in a row behind him. Many of the boys laughed nervously. Some of the girls cried.

As Officer Banks wound up the presentation, I took a few photos of the kids. It was then that I saw Tyler, the boy in the red hoodie with the skull on the back. The janitor's son. He peeked around the door to the gym.

I followed the wall behind the kids to reach him. As I did so, I heard Principal Sloan directing the students back to class over the intercom.

"Tyler," I said.

He turned to me, looking scared. "You're that reporter," he said. He held up both hands as if defending himself. "I heard kids saying I made that bomb threat, but I swear it wasn't me."

"Tyler, you've got to tell me the truth. Did you hide a bomb in this school or not?"

"God, no. Wait, there really is a bomb?"

Before I could answer, the students started pouring toward the gym exit. Kids bumped into us from every direction as they hurried out the gym door. Ashley glanced first at Tyler and then knowingly at me as she brushed past me. An instant later the boy with a pierced lip knocked me against the wall so hard that Tyler took my hand to help me keep my balance. "Freak," Tyler called after him. But Spider only sneered at Tyler.

"Spider, stop!" I said. "I need to talk to you!"

Then I felt a whoosh, as if I was plummeting down a tunnel. Suddenly I found myself alone in the school hallway. The kids had disappeared.

What the hell? I thought.

"Claire."

I swung around at the sound of the man's voice and found the janitor there in the hall with me. He wore his gray uniform and held a mop.

"We need to get to the furnace room—now." I felt odd as I said that, as if I was listening to someone else. Then I felt my body run down the stairs after the janitor, but I didn't feel in control. I felt like I was following myself.

As soon as the janitor opened the furnace-room door, I ran to the corner behind the furnace. There it was, a homemade pipe bomb hidden near the furnace. Wires attached a digital timer and a small ignition device to it. The bomb was about to go off. The timer clicked out the last few seconds on the screen. *Ten, nine, eight, seven...*

"We're out of time!" I cried. I turned and fled toward the door. But just then the boom of the explosion sounded, throwing me across the hall and against the wall. An instant later a ball of fire roared toward me, and I knew I was about to die.

SEVEN

jolted back to myself in a gym full of kids. My heart pounded in my chest. I was still alive! More to the point, I was back in the present. A moment before, I had visited my own future, a future in which I died.

"You okay?" Tyler asked me. "You zoned out. You need to see a doctor or something?"

I looked down at Tyler's hand holding my elbow. In the past, I had visions of a person when I held something they owned, like a piece of clothing. This time, Tyler had held my arm as I had the vision. So, I thought, Tyler *was* the bomber.

I dragged him toward Officer Banks. "Come with me," I said.

"I didn't tweet that bomb threat."

"Then you won't mind talking to the cops."

I led Tyler to the front of the gym and handed him over to Banks. "I believe you were looking for Tyler?"

Banks nodded. "We were. I've got some questions to ask you, young man."

As Banks interviewed Tyler, I pulled the chief to the side. "Jim, I know where the bomb is."

"Claire, for god's sake, there is no bomb. The sniffer dog didn't find any explosives."

"I'm telling you there *is* a bomb, and I know exactly where it is." I glanced at Tyler. I was nervous of getting another kid in trouble without proof. But then, Banks was already questioning him. "And I'm pretty sure Tyler is the bomber."

The chief watched me for a moment. "You had a vision."

"Yes, just now. I was talking to Tyler when it happened. He was holding my arm. Jim, the bomb is in the basement. It's a homemade pipe bomb with a timer. But the bomb is set right by the furnace. If that thing goes off—"

"It could blow this whole building, I know. Okay. Let me take it from here."

"But I've got to tell the cops what I saw."

The chief shook his head. "Claire, you know what they'll say."

"But we've got to get these kids out of here!"

Jim took me by both shoulders. "Claire, calm down. Let me handle this."

I took a deep breath and nodded. "Okay."

I watched the chief as he approached Officer Banks. Tyler looked panicked as he overheard what Jim had to say. Then Banks took the arm of the principal and spoke into her ear. She ran from the gym. Within moments I heard her voice over the school PA system.

"Teachers, please lead your students outside to the field by the nearest exit. This is not a drill. I repeat, this is not a drill. Everyone must leave the building immediately."

As the principal repeated the announcement, Banks appeared to give Tyler the okay to leave too. The boy fled from the gym. Then I saw the chief round up his team and talk briefly with the cops. When they all marched toward the gym door, I followed. Jim took me by the arm.

"Claire, you can't come with us. You need to wait outside with everyone else."

"But Chief, in my vision I saw exactly where the bomb is. It's hidden. They may not find it otherwise."

"The cops have the sniffer dog, and they know their job."

"You don't understand. I've got to help. I've got to be there." My voice rose loud enough that the cops turned at the gym door to look at me. "I was there in my vision."

"Claire!" Jim lowered his voice. "You're making a difficult situation worse. Please, just go outside."

But Banks was already striding toward us, anger hot on his face. "*That's* why you're sending us back to the basement?" he asked Jim. "Because Claire had a vision? You said you overheard some kids talking."

The chief's face reddened in embarrassment. So he had lied to help me, to help the kids.

"You've got to check the furnace room anyway," I said.

"Of course we will," Banks said. "We check out *all* bomb threats." He looked pointedly at me. Clearly he thought my warning about a bomb wasn't much different than the kid's bomb threat. I had already forced the cops to make a second sweep of the school. Now they had evacuated the school again.

"Get her out of here!" Officer Banks ordered.

One of the cops stepped forward to take my arm, but the chief waved him off. "I'll deal with her," he said.

"You do that," said Banks. He pointed a finger at Jim. "And don't waste our time like this again."

"The bomb has to be there," I said. "You don't understand what my visions are like. They aren't just gut feelings. I'm *there*. I saw the bomb explode. I died."

"Do you hear yourself?" Banks asked me.

"Let's go, Claire," the chief said quietly.

"But the bomb has to be there!"

"I said get her out of here!" Officer Banks yelled.

Jim's face was red as he dragged me out the door. I knew Banks and the other cops thought I was nuts. Worse, I knew I had embarrassed the fire chief in front of them.

Even so, I was convinced the dream and vision I had seen was of the future. A bomb *would* go off in that school.

EIGHT

I waited outside with the teachers and kids while the cops once again checked the furnace room. After a time the chief left the school and walked toward me. His face was grim.

"Did you find it?" I asked.

"Claire, there is no bomb. We searched every inch of that furnace room."

"But when Tyler held my arm, I saw the bomb there. I saw it explode."

"I believe you saw something," Jim said. "And I believe it's very real to you.

Your mother is always so sure about her visions. But when the cops check her tips, she's almost always wrong. Claire, I'm worried for you. You're a good reporter. You've built a name for yourself. Don't throw it away with this nonsense."

He was right. I had already lost Officer Banks's respect. That was a real problem, as I went to him for news stories about crimes in town. Still, I couldn't let this go.

"Please, Jim," I begged. "Don't let them send the kids back in until they find that bomb."

"Claire, they can't shut down the school indefinitely. And you know they can't shut down the school based on your hunch."

"My vision, my dream."

Jim crossed his arms as if I had made his point for him. Suddenly I saw things from his side. All Jim had to go on was my word. Why *would* he believe me?

"Jim, my visions helped Matt find Amber Miller and helped you stop that arsonist. That's got to count for something."

"Claire, let this go before you lose everything."

The chief turned on his heel and went back into the school. A few minutes later the cops allowed the students back in. By now it was almost lunchtime.

I couldn't let this go. I had lived through that explosion. I had died there. I wouldn't let any of these kids lose their lives.

As I watched the kids file back inside, I thought about the dream I'd had. In it, the janitor said he could help. Now I knew he was Tyler's father. Obviously, he wouldn't want his son responsible for a school bombing. If Tyler was the bomber in my vision, then maybe the janitor could help me stop him from setting off that bomb.

I slipped into the school through the side door, avoiding Banks and the other cops.

The hallway was empty, as the students were back in class at least until the noon bell rang. Ashley had said Tyler ate lunch with his dad in the furnace room. So the janitor was likely there now or would be soon. I made my way down the stairs to the basement.

The door to the furnace room was open. The janitor sat at a small table, drinking coffee with his lunch kit open beside him. He looked up, surprised, when I knocked and then entered.

"I'm Claire Abbott," I said. "I'm a reporter from the *Black Lake Times*." I held out my hand, but he refused to shake it.

I took out my cell to add his name to my contact list. "And your name?"

"Dean. But I've got nothing to say to you. I heard you were sniffing around, trying to blame my son for that bomb threat."

"I talked to a witness who overheard your son planning the threat."

"Well, your witness got it wrong. Yesterday afternoon Tyler heard Spider talking about posting a bomb threat on Twitter. Tyler confronted him, said it was a stupid thing to do. But he didn't want to get Spider in trouble, so he didn't say anything to me until after the last evacuation. I just told Principal Sloan about it."

"Maybe Tyler was covering his tracks by putting the blame on Spider."

"I know my son. He wouldn't lie to me."

"All teens lie to their parents."

"Not Tyler. He and I are close. I'm the only family he's got now. My wife died a year ago. Cancer. Her death hit him hard. That's why I took this job, so I'm around for him."

"I understand you have lunch with him here every day." I looked around the small, warm room. The furnace took up most of the space. There were no windows.

"Tyler's been keeping to himself since his mother died. I tried to get him to hang out with friends, but the school counselor said he needed time to grieve."

"So he has access to this furnace room. I imagine other kids don't."

"I keep the room locked most of the time. Look, what are you getting at?"

"I understand Tyler has taken an interest in model rockets."

Dean's face lit up for a moment. "Yes! It's the one thing he's enjoyed since his mom's death. I bought him several rockets. We launch them most weekends."

"So I'm right in thinking he does have all the materials to build a pipe bomb."

Dean's face darkened again. "He would never do that."

"Tyler ran into the building after the school was evacuated," I said. "He was the only kid who did that, like he knew there was no bomb. *Yet.*"

Dean stood up and leaned over the table. "He ran down to this basement, looking for me. In the rush to get out, I left my cell here." He pointed at the phone that sat on the table now. "Tyler panicked when he couldn't reach me and thought I was still inside. He was scared there might really be a bomb. He was trying to save my life."

"He could have told you that story to cover up what he was really doing, setting a bomb."

"The cops searched the school. It's clean. There is no bomb."

"Not yet."

"Not *yet*?"

I hesitated. "I see things. In visions," I admitted, feeling foolish. "Things that have happened or will happen. I had a dream where I saw a bomb go off. More than that, I *experienced* a bomb going off."

The janitor studied my face for a moment, then nodded. "My wife dreamed she would die long before the doctor told her she had breast cancer. I tried to tell her it was just a dream, but she knew different."

"I'm so sorry," I said.

"In this dream of yours," Dean asked, "did you see Tyler setting that bomb?"

"No, but I saw him run into the school minutes before it blew up. Also, he was holding my arm when I had the vision where I saw the bomb in this room. That makes me think Tyler may be the bomber. In the past, I've had visions when I held an object that belonged to the person involved."

Dean looked worried. "In your dream, did my son get out before the explosion?"

I paused. "I don't know. I hope so. I also saw you there."

"*Me*? You don't think *I'm* the bomber."

"No," I said. Then I thought about it. "You *are* happy in your job, right? No grudges against the school?"

Dean's face turned red with anger. "I would never hurt these kids."

"I've got to ask. You are one of the few people with a key to this furnace room. I saw that bomb go off here."

"In your *dream*."

"In my vision." I held out both hands. "Look, you just said your own wife dreamed about the future. Isn't it possible I did too?"

"I suppose."

"In the dream, you said you could help me."

"Help you? How?"

"Whether you want to believe it or not, your son is the most likely suspect at the moment. We have a witness who says he made that bomb threat. He eats lunch with you here. He could easily get his hands on the key to this room. All I'm asking is that you watch your son. Dean, I hope I'm wrong. But what if I'm right?"

Dean scratched the back of his neck. "Well, I did take the day shift at this school so I could keep tabs on him and be home every night."

"Then I know you *can* help me, just like you said in my dream."

A muffled voice echoed over the PA system on the floor above us. But we couldn't make out what the principal said. My cell chirped, and I pulled it from my pocket. "Ah, hell," I said after I read the text from my editor.

"What is it?" Dean asked.

"Some kid posted another bomb threat against this school on Twitter."

I heard footsteps coming down the hall, and the school principal entered the furnace room. She appeared surprised to see me down there. "You've got to leave the building," she said. "We're evacuating the school again."

I held up my phone. "We heard."

"The threat on that tweet said the bomb will go off as soon as lunch hour ends," she said.

The principal left, and I turned to Dean. "Has Tyler or anyone other than you had access to the furnace room after the cop and the sniffer dog were last here?"

"I left the door open for a few minutes while I used the washroom."

I glanced at the time on my cell. "If the bomb threat is for real, we're only got minutes to find the bomb and disarm it."

NINE

The first place I looked was behind the furnace. I had seen the bomb there in my vision. But there was no bomb. Dean and I searched the furnace room from top to bottom. I looked at my watch again. "Time is just about up. If there really is a bomb, it could blow any moment."

"We should get the hell out of here," Dean said.

I nodded. I didn't know what else to do. I followed Dean upstairs. He disappeared into a crowd of kids, looking for his son. I was surprised to see students were entering the halls from outside. Cop cars and fire trucks once again filled the school parking lot.

I saw Fire Chief Wallis in the hall outside the principal's office, talking to one of the cops. He was dressed in full fire-fighting gear. I pushed my way through the crowd of kids to reach him. "What's going on?" I asked Jim. "Why aren't you evacuating the kids?"

"We did, briefly. But then one of the students told us who made the threat on Twitter. The kid was stupid enough to post the threat on a school computer and then brag about it to the others in the room. The cops tracked him down, and he confessed. It's just another prank, Claire. There is no bomb."

"Was it that kid with the pierced lip? Spider?"

"Yeah, how did you know?"

"So Tyler may have been telling the truth," I said. "Maybe Tyler didn't make that first bomb threat this morning. Maybe it was Spider." Spider had bumped into me just before I had that vision in the hall. Maybe then it was Spider, and not the janitor's son, who had triggered my vision. "Where is Spider now?" I asked the chief.

"Officer Banks is questioning him in the office. Principal Sloan has called his parents."

"I've got to talk to that kid. *He* may be the one who will set that bomb, if he hasn't already."

"Claire, don't!" Jim called, but I was already heading into Principal Sloan's office.

Officer Banks stood as I rushed in.

"Claire, this is a private meeting," Principal Sloan said.

The chief caught up to me then. "I'm sorry," he said to Officer Banks. "I tried to stop her."

"I need to talk to this kid," I said.

Banks blocked my way. "No, you don't."

"Please, just let me touch him."

"*Touch* him?"

If I could just touch his arm, I might have a vision of what he was up to. I pushed past the cop and reached for Spider's arm. Even in that moment I knew what I must look like—a crazy woman lunging at this kid. Officer Banks grabbed my arm to stop me.

"What the hell are you doing?" he asked me.

"I need to know if he's the one who planted the bomb."

"No one accused him of making a bomb," said Principal Sloan. "He admitted to posting the bomb threat on Twitter. That's all."

"I didn't make a bomb," Spider said. "It was just a joke, you know? The last bomb threat wasted the morning. I wanted the afternoon off too."

"A bomb threat is deadly serious," Officer Banks said. "What if there was a real emergency—a fire or an accident—and we were stuck here making sure there was no bomb? Lives could be lost." He eyed me. "And *you* would be responsible."

I hung my head, feeling the heat of shame wash over me. Officer Banks clearly thought I was as reckless as this kid.

"Please wait outside," he said. As I stepped into the hall, he talked to both the principal and Fire Chief Wallis. I strained to hear what they were saying but couldn't.

Jim finally left the office and approached me. "Let's go," he said. He held my arm a little too hard as he pulled me through the crowd of kids toward the front entrance.

"Jim, what's going on?" I asked.

"Banks advised the admin to ban you from the school, and they have."

"Principal Sloan *banned* me?"

"You aren't allowed to step foot on school property."

"But I'm a reporter. I have to come up here when there's a school event. It's my job."

"I'm sorry, Claire. You're not allowed to be here."

"For how long?"

The chief led me outside. "Indefinitely," he said. "Given how you behaved today, I'm not sure they'll ever let you back."

"I can't believe this."

"Claire, you brought this on yourself."

"Jim, please, you've got to believe me. Someone *will* set a bomb in this school. Spider may have already. Unless we do something, this school will explode. All these students could die."

Jim led me to my car. "I did believe you, Claire. I stuck my neck out to protect you. Now I'm a laughingstock. You've not only ruined your own reputation. You've hurt mine too."

"I'm so sorry, Jim."

"Go home," the chief said. Then he headed back into the school.

Sitting around home was the last thing I wanted to do. I needed to bury myself in my work. I got in my car and drove to the newspaper office. I had lost the respect of both Fire Chief Wallis and Officer Banks. I knew I had lost my good name. At least, I thought, I still had my job.

TEN

I walked into the newspaper office feeling exhausted and defeated. "Well, look what the cat dragged in," my editor said.

I sat at my desk. "I'm sorry, Carol. I should have called."

"Or at least replied to my texts. I've got a paper to get out, you know."

"I've been working on this case."

"This *case*? Don't you mean a news story? Who do you think you are? A cop?"

I shook my head. "No, of course not. I was working on that bomb-threat story.

Carol, I really do think a bomber intends to blow up that school."

"Oh, I know all about it. I just got calls from both Officer Banks and the high-school principal."

"Crap." I held my head in both hands. I should have known Banks would phone Carol.

"They told me you are banned from the school," Carol said. "And not just the high school, but from every school in the district."

"Oh, no."

"Oh, yes. Claire, we run a small-town weekly. Big stories are few and far between. Most weeks we fill this paper with stories about community events, school plays and art shows. How are you going to do your job when you can't even step on school grounds?" She walked over and sat on my desk. "And how do you expect to get a story from the cops when they won't talk to you?"

"You're firing me?"

"I'm suspending you until this blows over."

I paused, taking in the anger on her face. "But you don't plan to hire me back, do you?"

"Can you blame me?"

"How are you going to fill the paper?"

"I have that intern coming, that co-op student. She can fill in for the moment."

"She wasn't due to start work until the end of April."

"I asked if she could start early, and she made arrangements. She'll be here in the morning."

"So that's it?"

"Pack up the things in your desk. I expect you to be out of here within the hour."

"I can't believe this is happening."

"Claire, I don't care how compelling your dreams and visions are. You can't go around claiming the school will blow up just because you dreamed it."

"But I *know* I'm right."

"Listen to yourself. You sound paranoid, delusional."

I nodded. "Crazy. I know."

Carol put a hand on my arm. "Claire, you're a good reporter. At least, you are when you aren't running around trying to solve crimes. Take some time to rest, clear your head." She strode back to her desk. "And for god's sake, get some help."

"I don't need a shrink."

"I think you do. A session with a counselor would do you a world of good."

I didn't reply. I couldn't convince her I was right about the bomber. I was even beginning to doubt myself. What proof did I have that the school would really explode? I had only a dream and a vision and this feeling of panic searing my gut.

I didn't need an hour to pack my things. My files filled only one box. Most of my work was on my laptop. I packed the computer in my camera bag and slung it over my shoulder. Then I picked up the box and faced Carol.

"I guess this is it," I said. I gulped hard to stop the tears.

"Claire, I still consider you my friend."

I felt the anger boil up. "How can you say that?" I headed for the door.

"Claire."

I turned back to her.

"Please," she begged. "Get some help."

I nodded once, then carried the box out of the office. I closed the door gently behind me and stood a moment in the hall to pull myself together. I didn't want the front-office staff to see me crying as I left, but the tears came anyway.

I had lost my reputation within my hometown. I had lost my friendship with Fire Chief Wallis. I had lost my job. But, I thought, at least I still had Matt. I wiped my tears with one hand and headed out the door.

ELEVEN

When I arrived at my apartment, Matt's truck was parked in front. He had let himself in with the key I had given him. The key to my apartment was a commitment of sorts. We weren't just dating anymore. He was my boyfriend now.

He opened the door to greet me. "I heard about what happened at the school," he said. "Chief Wallis phoned to say you were banned from school property. He was worried about you."

"Did you also hear I lost my job?"

"Oh, Claire, I'm so sorry." Matt wrapped his arms around me. He was a head and shoulders taller than me. In that moment I felt protected, and I sobbed in his arms.

"That school is going to explode, and no one believes me!"

Matt stepped back to hold my shoulders. "Claire, you can hardly fault the cops. You've given them nothing to go on except a hunch."

"You don't believe me either."

"I didn't say that."

"You didn't have to." I pushed past him into my apartment. Mom was there, sitting at the kitchen table. She stood when I came into the room. "Finally!" she said. "Maybe now you can tell me what's going on."

"I didn't think it was my place to tell her," Matt said. "But I thought you'd want her here."

I nodded. He was right. I needed to talk to Mom, and not just for her emotional support.

"Have you ever seen into the future?" I asked her.

Mom sat back down, her expression changing to concern. "No. I'm a remote viewer. I only see things as they are happening, in the present. What's going on?"

"I dreamed the school exploded." I decided against telling her that in the dream I died. "Mom, it was so real. Then there really was a bomb scare at the school this morning."

"They found a bomb?"

Matt shook his head. "Some kid made a bomb threat. I'm sure Claire picked up on the event. That's what her dream was about."

"No," I said to him. "There's more to it." I turned back to Mom. "Just after the assembly at the school, I had a vision. I saw a pipe bomb go off in the furnace room. The cops checked. There was nothing there."

"So you believe what you saw *will* happen, in the future."

"I'm sure of it." I sat down at the table with Mom. "I just don't know when. And I don't know what to do about it. I embarrassed the fire chief. Officer Banks won't listen to me."

Mom sighed. "He's stopped listening to me as well," she said. "Not that I blame him." Mom looked up at Matt. "What I see in my visions really is what's happening, you know," she said. "The thing is, by the time your search-and-rescue team gets there, the lost hiker has moved on. Or the body of the girl who drowned has already been swept downriver."

"So what do I do?" I asked her. "I know a bomb will blow up that school. I just don't know when."

"Do you have any idea who the bomber is?" Mom asked.

"The janitor's son, Tyler, has lunch in the furnace room. And he's into model rockets, so he has the knowledge and materials to make a pipe bomb."

"Well, there you go. You just need to watch that kid."

"It could also be the kid who admitted to making the bomb threat at lunchtime. Spider ran into me just before I had that vision. But then several other kids bumped into me as they left the gym."

"Think carefully," Mom said. "Who touched you immediately before you had that vision?"

"Well, like I said, Spider slammed into me. Tyler took my elbow to steady me. And just before that Ashley brushed by."

"Ashley?"

"She's the girl who first told Jim and me that Tyler made the bomb threat." I paused, thinking back on the day's events. "Oh my god," I said. "It never occurred to me that Ashley could be the bomber."

"Because she's a girl?" Matt asked.

"Yes, that's part of it," I said. "I just assumed the bomb threat was made by a boy. And Ashley looks like one of those girls who has money and friends. Tyler is a loner who just lost his mom, and he is into rockets." I looked up. "But then, so is Ashley. Matt, Ashley knows all about mixing the rocket-fuel chemicals into gunpowder. She knows how to make it into an explosive. And she knows how to connect that explosive to an igniter and timer. She learned how to do that for rockets in class, just like Tyler."

"I imagine everyone in her science class knows how."

"Yes, but she was quick to put the blame on Tyler. Maybe too quick, like she was trying to hide the fact that she made the bomb threat. She was also watching the cops and sniffer dogs from the fire trucks, far closer to the school than the other kids. And she watched them with almost too much interest. I think she's our bomber."

"But you don't have proof," Matt said.

"No, but we've got to make sure she never sets that bomb."

Matt shook his head in disbelief. "You're talking about catching a criminal before she's committed a crime. This is nuts, Claire."

"Maybe, but what if I'm right?"

"She was right about Amber Miller," Mom said. "Claire caught her kidnapper."

"And I caught the arsonist, Trevor. I stopped him from setting more fires."

Matt looked annoyed with me. "After you dated him."

"I know I've made mistakes. I'm not always sure what my visions are telling me. But Matt, if I don't stop Ashley, I *know* she will blow up that school."

"How many young lives might be lost?" Mom asked him.

Matt studied my face for a moment, then nodded. "Okay, so how are we going to stop the bomber?"

"You believe me?"

"I believe *in* you," he said. "If you believe this strongly in your vision, then I'll do whatever I can to help you." He pulled me back into his arms. "But we can't stand guard in front of the furnace room night and day. You're not even allowed on school property."

"That's why I need to get the janitor involved."

"Dean?" Matt asked.

I nodded. My dream had spelled it out. "I need the janitor's help."

"What can he do?"

"I'll show you," I said. I took Matt's hand. "Come on. I've got to pick up something in town. Then we'll head back to the school."

"You aren't allowed on the school grounds."

"But you are," I said.

TWELVE

I waited just outside the school grounds while Matt went inside the school. Classes were over for the day, and the kids were waiting outside for their buses to arrive. Within a few minutes Matt strode back toward me, with Dean following behind.

"You shouldn't be here," Dean said when he reached me. "You've been banned. I have to report you if I see you here."

"I know, and I know you have no reason to trust me." I glanced at Matt, hoping his support would get Dean on side. "But we need your help."

"Tyler is no bomber. He's a good kid."

"I believe you."

"You do?"

"I have reason to believe someone else may be planning to plant a bomb in the furnace room. I'm sure you would do everything you could to save the kids in this school."

"Of course."

"Does the school have surveillance cameras to watch for break-ins?"

"Yes, but just on the outside doors."

"So there is no camera in the basement."

Dean shook his head. "And if the bomber wanted to get away with it, he would have to plant the bomb during the day. The motion detectors in the school will sound the alarm at night."

I nodded. "We need a set of eyes on the furnace room." From my bag, I pulled out the two small web cameras I had just bought at the electronics store. "Can you install these cameras, one just outside the furnace room and one inside? They're wireless. I can pick up the camera images on my smartphone. That way I can stop the bomber."

"And have proof that what you've been telling everyone is for real," Matt said.

I nodded. I would have evidence to take to Officer Banks, to Chief Wallis and to my editor. "Dean, you'll have to make sure the cameras are hidden, maybe under a light fixture. And you understand you can't tell Tyler about them. We can't tell *anyone* about these cameras. If we do, word could spread. Principal Sloan would undoubtedly put an end to this plan."

"Or the real bomber might remove the cameras." Dean sighed. "I get it."

He did seem to understand. I just hoped my trust in him wasn't misplaced. He still might report me to the principal.

I turned to Matt. "We'll have to take turns watching around the clock.

You'll have to keep an eye on my phone when I grab a nap."

Matt nodded. "I'm up for it."

"I'll have to stay at your place until all this plays out," I said. "Your house is only minutes from the school."

Matt grinned. "I can live with that."

"But what if you really did dream of the future?" Dean asked me. "My wife dreamed about her own death. There was nothing we could do to stop it from happening. What if we can't stop this bomb from going off?"

"I have to believe there is a reason why I had that nightmare and that vision," I said. "We *have* to stop this from happening." If I couldn't, so many lives would be lost, my own among them.

THIRTEEN

I woke in the morning to a gentle push on my shoulder. "Hey, sleepyhead."

"Matt," I said, looking up into his rugged face. I sat up, still feeling groggy. "What time is it?" I had tossed and turned all night.

"Just about nine."

"Nine?" I glanced at the bright light streaming through the window. "You were supposed to wake me in the night so you could get some sleep."

"After the day you had yesterday, I figured you needed the rest more than I did."

"You stayed up all night?"

"Someone had to keep an eye on that bomber." He handed me my smartphone. "Nothing to report. All clear in the furnace room."

"I'm so sorry, Matt. How are you going to get your work done?"

He pushed my curls away from my face. "I'll be fine. I can catch a nap in my office if I need to." He patted my leg. "I've got to get going. There's a plate of eggs and toast on the table."

He kissed me, and I grew shy. I wasn't used to having a man take care of me this way. "I don't know how to thank you, for everything," I said. "For believing in me."

He grinned. "I'm sure you'll think of something. Later?"

"Later."

I watched him leave the room and heard the front door close behind him. Then I got out of bed and dressed in jeans and a T-shirt.

Breakfast was waiting on the kitchen table as Matt promised. I held the coffee cup in my hands as I watched the image on my cell phone. Matt was right. Nothing to report. Just an empty furnace room with the light left on. I checked the other web camera. All I saw was an empty hallway and closed furnace-room door. I was grateful, but I almost wished the bomber would act. The waiting was unbearable.

Then, all at once, my wait was over. Oh my god! I thought. The bomber was Tyler after all! I saw him approach the furnace room. He unlocked the door with his father's set of keys and went inside. I switched the view to the inside camera and watched as he went over to the table. He picked up both his lunch kit and his father's, then left the room, locking the door behind him.

I sat back in my chair and breathed a sigh of relief. Tyler was only spending his free block with his dad in the cafeteria. Dean had agreed to eat there and keep the furnace room locked until the bomber had been caught.

The minutes ticked by. I had more coffee, cleaned up after breakfast, then checked the time on my cell phone. It was just about ten.

I flipped the view back to the camera facing the furnace-room door. There was a figure at the door, someone wearing a black hoodie with the hood up. Was it Ashley, or was it Spider? This kid was dressed like Spider, all in black.

The person turned to look down the hall, and I finally saw her face. Ashley! She jimmied the furnace-room door open. She had broken in!

"Shit." As I rushed to the car, I flipped my cell screen to the camera image from inside the furnace room. Ashley pulled an object from a duffel bag. A pipe bomb.

I hit Matt's name on my contact list as I started the car. He picked up the call after two rings. "Matt, Ashley *is* the bomber! She's in the furnace room right now. I'm on my way over, but once I get there I'm not sure the staff will listen to me. I know the cops won't."

"Okay, hang on. I'll be right there. Have you phoned Dean?"

"Not yet." Of course, Dean. In my panic, my first thought had been to phone Matt. I hung up and dialed the janitor's number. But his phone went to voice mail.

"Damn it."

I flipped back to the image from the furnace-room camera. Sure enough, Dean's cell phone was sitting on the table. He'd forgotten to take it with him at this of all times. Ashley was still in the furnace room, setting up the bomb. I was only five minutes from the school, but that might be five minutes too long. I had to get the principal to stop her.

As I pulled out of the apartment parking lot, I dialed the school. The receptionist picked up. "Black Lake High School."

"There's a bomb," I said as I drove. "In the furnace room. Ashley is in there right now setting up a pipe bomb. I'm on my way, but you've got to stop her."

"Who is this?"

I hesitated. "Claire Abbott. I work for the newspaper." Or at least I did. "Please, tell the principal and phone the cops."

"You've been banned from school property for just this kind of behavior," she said.

"I know. But there really is a bomb. I'm not making this up."

"That's what you said last time." She hung up.

"Shit!" I threw the phone on the seat and pressed the gas pedal to the floor.

FOURTEEN

I brought the car to a halt right in front of the main school entrance and ran for the door. But Principal Sloan was there waiting for me, barring the way. She was dressed in a pink pantsuit, but she still managed to look intimidating.

"You've been told to stay off school property," she said.

"You've got to evacuate the kids, *now!*"

"The police are on their way."

"Good," I said. "But they may be too late. We've got to stop Ashley now."

"Ashley?" she said. "I called the cops to deal with you."

"We put cameras in the furnace room. She's in the basement right now, setting a bomb."

"You did what?"

"I had to. It was the only way. There's no time to explain." I tried to push past her, but she grabbed my arm. "Let me go!" I said. "I've got to stop that bomb from going off!"

I struggled out of her grip and rushed through the school door. I found myself alone in the school hallway. The kids were in their classes. The doors to the rooms were closed.

"Claire."

I swung around and found Dean, the janitor, there in the hall with me.

"We need to get to the furnace room now." I held up my smartphone. "It was Ashley. I saw her set that bomb."

As the principal reached us she said to Dean, "Help me get Claire out of here before the kids hear her."

Dean looked from the principal to me and back again. "No," he said. "We've got to get down to the furnace room, *now*."

He pulled out his keys as he ran down the stairs to the basement. As I followed, I heard the wail of a police car heading our way. The principal trailed behind us.

As soon as the janitor opened the furnace-room door, I ran to the corner of the room. There I found the bomb exactly where I had seen it in my vision. To my horror, I also saw we had less than ten seconds before the bomb went off. "We're out of time!" I cried.

In my vision I had turned and fled at this moment. If I hadn't run, there may have been enough time to disarm the bomb. I made a split-second decision. Instead of fleeing, I crouched down beside the bomb. The digital timer rigged to the bomb ticked out the last few seconds before it was set to blow. *Five, four, three, two...*

FIFTEEN

I yanked the timer from the bomb. The wires that had run to the igniter dangled from it. I held my breath, convinced the bomb would still go off. But there was no boom, and I was still alive. I let my breath go, relieved.

"You did it!" Dean cried. He took my hand and helped me up. Principal Sloan blinked at me, confused. "How?" she stuttered. "Who?"

"We still need to get out of here," I said. "This bomb could still go off. You've got to evacuate the school. *Now.*"

She nodded and fled up the stairs with Dean and me right behind her. I heard her voice over the PA system as Dean and I knocked on classroom doors and led kids out the front entrance.

Officer Banks rushed into the parking lot in his police car, siren blaring. Moments later Matt parked immediately behind the police car. Both Matt and the cop ran to the front of the building, where Dean, the principal and I continued to direct students out the door.

Matt hugged me. "Oh, thank god," he said. "You're all right."

"We just got a call there was another bomb threat," Officer Banks said to the principal. Then he turned to me, looking angry. "That wasn't you, was it?"

"No, it was me," said Matt.

"There really is a bomb in the furnace room." I held out the timer. "I just disarmed it." I paused. "I think."

"Is she telling the truth?" Officer Banks asked the principal. She nodded. The cop immediately phoned the bomb squad. It was then that I saw Ashley, watching the evacuation from the far end of the parking lot. But I pretended I hadn't seen her, for the moment.

As Banks ended his call, I said, "Ashley set the bomb."

"Are you sure?"

I showed him my smartphone. He watched the video of Ashley breaking into the furnace room and setting the bomb. "And she's right over there," I said.

As soon as I pointed at her, Ashley turned and bolted. Officer Banks scrambled to catch her. He nabbed her as she ran down the side-walk, then hauled her back to his police car. Once there, he pulled her hands behind her back and slapped the cuffs on her.

"I want to phone my lawyer," she said.

"You have your own lawyer?" I asked.

"My family does."

"The first thing we're going to do is phone your parents," Officer Banks said.

"My parents?" Ashley shook her head. "It'll be days before my parents get here. My mom is on another business trip in New York. My dad is on holiday with his new family in Costa Rica."

"Who is responsible for you then?" I asked. "Who is staying with you?"

"Our housekeeper."

"Your *housekeeper*?" I repeated.

"She was my nanny." Ashley shrugged. "Mom is hardly ever around."

I realized her housekeeper was likely the closest thing to a parent this girl had. I was suddenly grateful for my loopy mom. After my parents divorced, she had built her home business so she would always be around for me. We didn't have much money, but I always had her attention and love.

"You made that first bomb threat, didn't you?" I asked Ashley.

Ashley looked down, caught. "Yeah, so?"

"You put the blame on Tyler. Why him? Why not Spider?"

She shrugged. "You had already picked him out as a suspect. He's a nerd. Keeps to himself. Nobody cares about him."

"His dad cares," I said. I glanced back to the field where Dean had joined his son. He put an arm around Tyler and nodded at me.

Ashley looked sad. I knew she felt her parents didn't care about her. Not enough to be around when she needed them. In that moment I almost felt sorry for her. But then her expression turned to anger. "The bomb was *your* idea, you know," she said to me.

I took a step back. "Mine?"

"I hadn't thought of planting a bomb in that school," Ashley said. "But then you thought there actually *was* one." She looked smug. "Then I heard you talked the cops and firefighters into going down to the furnace room to look for the bomb. I realized that was the perfect place to plant a pipe bomb. If it set off the fuel in the furnace, the explosion would be *way* bigger. But the bomb wasn't near a classroom, so no one would get hurt."

Officer Banks put a hand on Ashley's shoulder. "If that bomb went off in the furnace room, the whole school could have gone up in flames. Many kids would have died."

Ashley's face went white as she finally understood what she'd done. "Well, it was her idea, not mine," she said, nodding at me. "It's *her* fault."

I felt sick to my stomach. I had been so sure I was seeing into the future. I had tried to stop the explosion from happening. Instead, I'd had a hand in creating the situation.

"Come on, into the car." Banks held Ashley's head so she wouldn't hit it as he helped her into the back of the police cruiser. He closed the car door behind her, locking her in.

"That is one sick kid," Matt said.

"But she's right. All those students could have died, and it would have been my fault."

Banks shook his head. "Don't let that kid get under your skin," he said. "Remember, she made that first bomb threat. And you certainly didn't talk her into making that pipe bomb."

Maybe, but I also knew I would never really be sure I had seen into the future. Had I stopped the explosion from happening? Or had I planted the seed in Ashley's mind, setting off this chain of events?

I glanced at Ashley. She turned away and stared straight ahead. She didn't look so cocky now.

SIXTEEN

The fire trucks arrived and the bomb squad entered the building. As Matt made a few calls, I watched with Tyler and Dean as the bomb squad carefully removed the pipe bomb from the school and loaded it into a special truck. Then the cops made another sweep of the school with the sniffer dog. When Officer Banks was sure the school was safe, he gave the okay to let the students back in. It was only then, after the cops and fire crews had left, that Matt and I finally left the school ourselves.

"Let's grab a coffee," Matt said. "I'll drive."

I got in his truck and we headed down-town. Matt parked opposite Tommy's Café, the local hangout for cops and firefighters.

"No, not here," I said. I glanced in the window. "The cops and firefighters are all in there. Fire Chief Wallis is there too. I embarrassed him."

"You've got to face him sometime. Now is as good a time as any."

"I guess." Matt was right. Still, my knees felt like jelly as I got out of the truck.

I took a deep breath and pushed open the café door. As I entered, everyone turned toward me. One of the firefighters slapped Fire Chief Wallis on the shoulder so he would turn to see me. The chief paused a moment as he caught my eye.

Then he stood and clapped. One by one, every cop and fireman in that café stood and clapped. Even the servers stopped working and cheered for me.

"Are they making fun of me?" I asked Matt.

"No, they're applauding you," Matt said. "You saved a lot of kids' lives today—*their* kids." He nodded at the crowd that surrounded us. Then he stood back and clapped along with them.

I felt the tears start to rise. Then I felt a hand on my shoulder. I turned to find my mother there. "What are you doing here?" I asked her.

She smiled at Matt. "I heard there was a little party here in your honor."

"You planned this?" I asked Matt. "Is *this* why you made all those calls earlier?"

"We all planned this," the chief said. He raised his coffee mug. "To Claire!" he said.

Everyone in the café raised a cup and joined him. "To Claire!"

The firefighting team lined up to shake my hand, followed by the cops. Officer Banks was the last to congratulate me.

"Claire, I was thinking we may hire you to help us on the occasional case," he said.

"Seriously?"

"You've proven yourself."

"You have a budget for hiring a psychic?"

He laughed. "I think I can get away with it if I call you a consultant."

"Maybe you can make use of my skills as well?" Mom asked.

"Mom," I warned.

Officer Banks turned to her. "I will take your calls from now on," he said. "And I'll listen to what you have to say."

"That's all I ever wanted," Mom said.

Officer Banks tipped his police hat and joined the other cops at his table. Carol, my editor, took that as her cue to approach me.

"Claire, I have an apology to make," she said. "I've known you long enough that I should have trusted you."

"No apology necessary," I said. "You had no reason to believe me. In the future, I'll make sure I have the facts to back my story before I bring it to you or the cops."

"Like any good reporter. Your job is open, if you still want it."

I grinned. "I've got to pay the bills somehow."

"See you tomorrow then?"

Matt wrapped an arm around my shoulder. "I think she deserves a day off after all this, don't you?"

Carol nodded. "I agree."

"What did you have in mind?" I asked Matt.

"I'll think of something." He winked, and I knew we'd be spending the day in bed. I was grateful. Aside from what else he had in mind, I could use a good sleep. This time, hopefully, without nightmares.

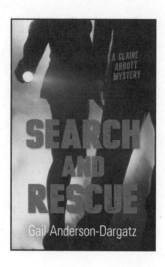

When a young woman goes missing on a nature trail, small-town journalist Claire Abbott is first on the scene, as usual. The clues to the woman's whereabouts are misleading, but Claire has a sixth sense—what the fire chief calls a "radar for crime." She's more than just a journalist chasing a story. Claire is determined to do the right thing at any cost.

   Search and Rescue is the first novel in a series of mysteries featuring journalist and sleuth Claire Abbott.

"[A] relatable character, and [Claire's] psychic ability grows at just the right pace for a short series opener." —*Booklist*

RAPID READS
WWW.RAPID-READS.COM

Small-town journalist Claire Abbott has a sixth sense, what the fire chief calls a "radar for crime." When a string of suspicious fires breaks out in town, Claire thinks she knows who the firebug is. Or does she? She finds there is much more to the story than she imagined. Worse, no one will believe her. The firebug is getting bolder, and the fires he sets more dangerous. Claire is now in a race against time to catch the arsonist in the act before he takes a life.

Playing with Fire is the second in a series of mysteries featuring journalist and sleuth Claire Abbott.

"An entertaining, accessible mystery."
—*School Library Journal*

RAPID READS
WWW.RAPID-READS.COM

By the age of eighteen, **GAIL ANDERSON-DARGATZ** knew she wanted to write about women in small-town and rural settings. Today, Gail is a bestselling author. *A Recipe for Bees* and *The Cure for Death by Lightning* were finalists for the Scotiabank Giller Prize. She also teaches other authors how to write fiction. Gail divides her time between the Shuswap region of British Columbia and Manitoulin Island in Ontario.

Race Against Time is the third book in the Claire Abbott Mystery series. For more information, visit gailanderson-dargatz.ca.